THE WITCH'S BREW

AN EROTIC FAIRYTALE

VICTORIA RUSH

VOLUME 4

CLOVER'S FANTASY ADVENTURES -
BOOK 4

COPYRIGHT

For the uninhibited...

WANT TO AMP UP YOUR SEX LIFE?

Sign up for my newsletter to receive more free books and other steamy stuff. Discover a hundred different ways to wet your whistle!

Victoria Rush Erotica

1

———

After Clover and her friends bade farewell to their dragons on the island of Sappho, they headed southward along the coastline, foraging in the woods for wild game and buried tubers. It wasn't the sumptuous feast they'd grown accustomed to on the island, but they were happy to be together again, looking for their next adventure. As she walked along the steep cliffs above the shore, Clover stared longingly out to sea.

"Are you missing our friends?" Tara said, noticing Clover's pensive mood.

"You mean Rex and Betty?" she said, referring to their pet dragon names. "It sure made moving around a lot easier. My feet are killing me."

"They'll be happier fending for themselves," Tara said. "Dragons weren't mean to be domesticated. Soon they'll be raising a family of their own, and we'd just be a distraction."

She paused as she peered out at the setting sun on the horizon.

"We should stop soon and put in for the night. Let's look

for some wood to build a fire, then try to catch some rabbits and quail for dinner."

"I'm going to miss our big feasts around the campfire," Jessop said, following the girls along a narrow trail into the forest. "What I'd do for some fresh grouper baked in lime juice right now."

"Are those the *only* juices you're going to miss from the island of Sappho?" Clover smiled.

"Probably not," he said, adjusting his crotch. "Those tribeswomen really knew how to satisfy our every need. I'm going to miss being the only man surrounded by a group of sex-starved beauties."

"Is your blood beginning to recirculate to your lower extremities?" Tara chuckled, noticing the bulge in his pants. "I thought after a week of non-stop orgies that you needed a rest?"

"It seems to be feast or famine with our adventures," Jessop grinned. "If I had to choose between the two, I'd rather have too much sex than too little."

"Don't worry, sport," Clover said, winking at Tara. "I'm sure between the two of us, we can help satisfy your needs. You're not the *only* one missing all that girly attention."

Suddenly Tara stopped along the path, holding up her hand as she crouched for cover.

"Do you hear that?" she said, peering back at her friends.

"Yes," Clover said, pinching her eyebrows. "It sounds like–"

"Someone having sex," Jessop nodded.

"But what's that *other* sound?" Tara said. "It sounds like some kind of animal..."

The three friends pulled the brush aside and peered through the branches at some moving figures in a clearing thirty feet away. A pretty nymph with lilac-colored hair was bent over next to a fire pit while a tall, heavily built man was humping his hips against her ass. But instead of the normal head of a human, the man had the head and long tail of a bull.

"What the–" Clover said, tripping backwards in surprise, snapping a twig.

The two figures in the clearing suddenly turned around and the man-bull disengaged, revealing an enormous penis with a thick, bulbous head.

"Who's there?" the woman said, standing up.

She motioned for the man to investigate, and as he approached their position, Jessop pulled his sword from its sheath while Tara placed an arrow in her bow, pointing it in the direction of the creature.

"Stop right there!" Jessop said, shaking his sword at the beast as it broke through the clearing and advanced toward them on the path.

The animal tilted its head, not knowing what to make of the intruders, and as it continued moving closer, Tara pulled her string back, preparing to strike him in the chest.

"Wait!" the purple-haired woman said, emerging onto the path a few feet behind the man. "Don't hurt him! He doesn't mean you any harm."

"That's not what it looks like to us," Tara said, holding her bow taut while she peered up at the hulking creature.

"He doesn't know any better," the woman said. "He's just defending his territory like any animal would."

"What kind of creature *is* that exactly?" Clover said, staring at the still tumescent enormous organ dangling between his legs.

"He's a minotaur," the woman said.

"But how–?" Tara said, shaking her head as she felt a strange tingling between her legs.

"Join us for dinner and I'll explain," the woman said. "You can put those weapons away, he won't hurt you.

"Come, Darius," she said, motioning for the man-beast to return to her side.

He looked at her, then back toward the three friends, then sauntered back toward the mysterious woman, kneeling at her feet while she petted his giant head.

As the trio followed the strange pair back to their campsite, Jessop peered at the two girls with a worried expression.

"Are you sure this is a good idea?" he said, watching the beast's tail swinging behind him as he plodded up the path.

"Something tells me it's better to make friends than *enemies* of these two," Tara said, holding her bow defensively by her side. "Besides, there's three of us and only two of them, and we have weapons."

"More like two and a *half* of them," Jessop said, staring at the large curved horns atop the creature's head. "He seems to have plenty of weapons."

"Are you referring to his pointy horns or his giant *penis*?" Clover chuckled. "Don't tell me you're getting *jealous* of this beast."

"Hardly," Jessop said, glancing around the woods. "But who's to say what other strange creatures this woman is keeping for pets?"

When they reached the fire pit in the clearing, the woman motioned for the group to sit on a log while she poured some stew into a large bowl and passed it around.

"Who are you?" Tara said, tipping the bowl up to her nose before taking a sip of the hearty broth. "And what are you doing with this...*creature*?"

"Wasn't it obvious while you were watching us through

the branches?" she smiled. "My name's Bronwyn, and I'm a witch. Sometimes a woman needs to satisfy her needs..."

"Okay, but why with a half man, half bull?"

"Why *not*?" the witch smiled. "Normal men can be so feeble and predictable. This one's strong and well-endowed, and does whatever I train him to do."

"And what exactly is that?" Clover said, still staring at the beast's organ bouncing between his legs while he peered at the two girls.

"Whatever I *want*," the witch smiled. "I see that you're intrigued, judging by the way you're looking at his penis and squirming on your log."

"Um, not really–" Clover stammered, peering up at the creature's flaring nostrils. "It's just that I've never seen anything like him before. He's so–"

"*Big?*"

"Well, yes," Clover said. "In more ways than one. Are you able to create your sex partners in whatever form you choose?"

"It depends on the material I have to work with," the witch said, drifting her eyes over toward Jessop, who was staring at the creature's oversize cock enviously. I can't turn men into female creatures or women into male creatures. But to some degree, the subject has to want the trans-formation."

"Is it *permanent*?" Tara said, passing the bowl along to her hungry friends.

"Usually only for a day or two," the witch said. "But they have to *perform* in order to return to their previous state."

"You mean...?" Clover said, admiring the minotaur's muscular and sinewy human-shaped body.

"*Exactly,*" the witch smiled. "Otherwise, what's the point? Animals are generally only good for two things."

Clover peered at the woman with a furrowed forehead, not sure what she meant.

"Food and fucking," the witch chuckled.

"That seems a bit harsh," Clover said. "We've found certain animals can make excellent companions."

"Like I said," the witch nodded, stroking the inside of the man-bull's thigh as his organ continued to swell.

"I didn't mean that way..."

"You never know until you *try*," the witch said, squeezing his hardening pole in her fist. "Darius seems quite taken with you. Would you like to see for yourself?"

"I prefer to stick with my own kind," Clover said, nodding toward Jessop sitting beside her, gulping down the soup. "Something with a *human* head."

"Suit yourself," the witch smiled, glancing toward Jessop's lower body.

Suddenly, his body began twitching as he rose higher on the stump and his feet turned into rounded hooves. While he peered at the rest of the group with a confused expression, the seat of his pants suddenly tore open as his backside extended behind him, growing a second pair of legs in the form of a horse's torso.

"What the fuck?" he said, looking down at his fur-covered lower body and bucking his hind legs awkwardly. "What have you done to me!"

"I saw you looking at Darius's penis enviously," the witch said. "And your girlfriend said she preferred something with a human head. So I thought I'd give you *both* something you can enjoy."

"Turn him back *immediately*!" Tara said, leaping up off the log and pointing her bow toward the witch and the bull.

"I can't," the witch said. "Like I said, once a person is

transformed, they have to meet certain requirements before they can return to their former shape."

"You intend to have *sex* with him like that?" Tara said.

"Actually," the witch said, tilting her head to glance at Jessop's hind quarters. "I was thinking one of *you* might want to take a turn with him. His animal instincts seem to already be taking over."

Tara and Clover turned toward Jessop and peered between his rear legs, noticing his horse cock pushing out of its sheath, lengthening to the size of his forearm.

"*Jessop!*" Tara said, staring at his enormous pink erection. "What the hell are you thinking?"

"I'm not thinking of anything," he said, shaking his head in dismay. "This thing seems to have a mind of its own."

"This is totally unacceptable," Tara said, turning back to the witch. "You can't just go around turning innocent people into horny woodland creatures!"

"Like I said," Bronwyn smiled. "I can only transform people who've already been thinking about it. You never know, maybe your boy will *enjoy* having a horse-sized cock for a change."

Tara paused as she looked at the witch incredulously.

"And the only way to return him to his previous form is to have *sex* with him?"

"It doesn't have to be *you* necessarily," the witch smiled. "Perhaps he'd be just as happy fucking another horse. Judging by the drip from his flaring cock, it looks like he could fuck just about anything at this point."

Clover and Tara peered between his hind legs, staring at his enormous bobbing pole.

"Holy fuck, Jessop!" Clover said. "That thing is *huge*!"

"And I don't exactly see another *horse* around here for him to mate with," Tara said, shaking her head.

Clover turned to the witch, suddenly feeling her pussy moistening while she stared at her friend's twitching organ.

"Does it matter how he, um, *mates* to remove the spell?" she said.

"Not really," the witch smiled. "As long as he finishes. But if he did it in the conventional way, it would likely work faster."

"I'm not exactly sure there's a *conventional* way to fuck a horse..." Clover said.

"You're not actually considering–?" Tara said, staring at Clover with wide eyes.

"Not in the usual way," Clover said. "I don't think that thing would fit inside me. Maybe I could stimulate him with my *hands* if that's all it takes."

"Like you're milking a *cow*?" Tara said, turning to glare at the witch. "Where do you come up with these perverted ideas?"

"It looks like I'm not the *only* one intrigued with the idea of having sex with an animal," the witch smiled as she watched Clover kneel under Jessop's belly and touch his twitching erection. "Why don't you watch and enjoy? You never know, maybe you'll want to try it next."

"Not in a million years," Tara said, nevertheless unable to stop watching Clover grasp Jessop's giant pole with both hands and begin rubbing them back and forth along his long length.

"It's actually not as bad as it seems," Clover said, staring at the flat head of his instrument with wide eyes. "It almost feels like a regular cock–just much longer. But the head is shaped differently..."

As she rolled her hand over the tip of Jessop's shaft, he grunted, rocking his hind quarters more vigorously into Clover's tight grip.

"Oh my God, Clover," he panted. "That feels incredible. Jerk my big horse cock. This feels three times as good as usual."

"Maybe that's because you're three times as *big*," she smiled, reaching out to caress his gigantic horse balls.

"Holy fuck!" he panted. "You're going to make me come if you keep doing that. You might want to get out of the way when I explode. I'll probably eject three times as much *cum* as well."

While Clover continued caressing Jessop's giant dick and balls, she turned to look at the witch, who'd impaled herself again on her man-bull's equally hard dick as they both sat on the log facing the couple.

"Can these creatures *impregnate* a human with their seed?" Clover said, watching them copulate. "What if–?"

"Knock yourself out," the witch grunted as she hopped up and down on the bull's fat prick. "He can only reproduce with those of his own kind. And since there's no other horses around, I'd say you're pretty safe."

"What do you say, stud?" Clover said, leaning over from under Jessop's belly and peering up at his face. "If I assume the position, do you think you can be gentle with me?"

"As gentle as one can be inserting a square peg into a round hole," he said. "As long as you're properly lubed up, I should be able to get at least *part* of it inside you."

"Are you guys fucking *crazy*?" Tara said, still staring at her two friends in disbelief.

"Possibly," Clover said, beginning to pull off her sheepskin vest. "But if there's only one way to return Jessop back to normal, we might as well make the most of it. I don't know about you, but I'm getting seriously turned on with all this male testosterone floating around in the air."

When she pulled all her clothes off, she bent down on

all fours, then tilted her ass up toward Jessop's cock, pulling his flaring tip toward her hole. As he pressed his tool against her dripping folds, she moved it from side to side until the thick tip penetrated her slit.

"Oh my God," Clover panted, feeling Jessop's cock slowly sliding into her wet hole. "I see what Bronwyn meant when she mentioned trying something different for a change. Three times the size really *is* three times as good."

"I told you you'd like it," the witch grinned, stroking Darius's big balls while she bobbed up and down with her legs spread wide apart. "Fuck Jessop's big dick and let him come inside you. You've never experienced a proper fucking until you've been filled with horse semen."

"*Yes*, Jessop," Clover panted, clutching onto some roots to keep herself from being pushed forward while he plowed his dick into her ass. "Fuck me hard and come inside my pussy. I don't suppose you're thinking about those sexy Sappho women any longer, are you?"

"Just when I thought it couldn't get any better," he grunted, clenching his fists against the side of his hairy flanks. "You better get ready, because I'm going to come like a firehose."

"Let it go," Clover said, grasping the bottom of his hooves for support. "Sink that dick all the way inside me. I'm going to come with you—"

"*Unghh!*" Jessop suddenly growled, pounding his hips forward, pressing Clover's face into the dirt. "Oh my God, Clover! This feels *insane*. I'm cumming so hard inside your pussy."

"I feel it, baby," Clover grunted, beginning to spray her juices out of the side of her tight cunt all over his quivering balls. "I'm cumming with you! I've never felt anything like this in all my life!"

While Clover and Jessop bucked against one another in mutual ecstasy, Bronwyn started screaming along with them as Darius thrust his twitching member deep inside her pussy, pulling her hard against his heaving chest.

After everybody finished grunting and moaning, they peered over at an unusually quiet Tara, who was squeaking softly as she rubbed her fingers rapidly between her legs.

It appears I'm not the only one who enjoys the idea of animal sex, Clover smiled to herself.

2

———

When Tara saw that everyone was watching her touching herself, she withdrew her hands from between her legs and sat back down sheepishly on the fireside log.

"You seemed to enjoy that more than you were letting on," Bronwyn smiled, noticing the wet spot in her tight-fitting suit.

"It's just that I've never seen anything like that before," Tara said, still gawking at Jessop's half-erect, huge, dripping horse organ.

"Do you get turned on at the thought of having sex with animals?"

"Not so much *with* an animal..." Tara said, recalling how Jessop described it feeling so much better than in his human form.

"Oh?" the witch said, walking toward Tara. "What kind of animal do you think you'd like to be?"

"I've never thought about it before," she said, wrinkling her nose at Darius's minotaur head. "Something that still makes me look like a girl at least–"

Bronwyn sat down on the log next to Tara and began running her hands through her silken hair. Tara peered back at her, momentarily transfixed by her gaze, then the two women thrust their tongues into each other's mouths, groaning as they intertwined their bodies. Suddenly, Tara's hair began moving atop her head, slowly morphing into a pile of snakes while her lower body melded together into the long, twisting body of a serpent.

"What the *hell*?" Clover said, stepping toward the amorous couple. "That hardly looks like a *girl*. What have you done to my friend? Turn her back immediately! She doesn't even have a–"

"*Pussy?*" the witch said. "How do you think snakes reproduce? Every animal has a male or a female part somewhere. It's just that hers is hidden from view."

Bronwyn drifted her hand down Tara's lower body, pressing two fingers into a small hole on the side of her belly. Suddenly, Tara's hair began writhing excitedly atop her head as she wrapped her tail around the witch's hips, pressing the small rattle at the tip into her slit.

"You see?" Bronwyn grunted, feeling Tara's rattle shaking inside her hole. "Snakes can have just as much fun as any other animal. You don't see her complaining, do you?"

While the rest of the group watched the two women twisting and probing each other, the men's penises began to grow once again in excitement. Darius wrapped his hands around his organ, and, feeling a new tingling between her legs, Clover approached the minotaur and knelt down between his legs, licking the tip of his flaring head with her tongue. Jessop's penis had been too large for her to get her lips around, but Darius's man-sized instrument looked hungry for the picking, and she eagerly engulfed his prick in her mouth as he grunted in approval.

"I *knew* Darius had his eye on you," Bronwyn grinned, tilting her hips forward to sink Tara's twitching tail deeper inside her pussy. "Do you like sucking his bull cock?"

"Mmm," Clover hummed, reaching between her legs to diddle her dripping sex.

"What about *you*, Jessop?" the witch smiled, noticing Jessop watching the others while he rubbed his huge prick in the grass as he knelt his hind legs on the ground. "Don't you want to get in on the action?"

"*Fuck* yes," he said, watching Clover sucking Darius's big cock with wide eyes. "It's just that all the openings seem to be occupied at the present time..."

"Not *all* of them," Bronwyn smiled, tilting her head in the direction of Darius and Clover. "Why don't you amble over there and see if you can find some *other* way to deploy that big horse cock?"

Jessop stared at Clover's ass resting on the ground as she bobbed her head up and down on Darius's pole, then he pranced over to her, rubbing his dick along the length of her back. She tried to reach behind her head to fondle his tip, but he was still too low for her to reach.

"Put your legs over her shoulders," Bronwyn said, watching him vainly trying to create friction with his penis stroking her back. "There's more than *one* way to stimulate that giant prick of yours."

Jessop lifted his front legs over Clover's back and his weight pushed her lower on Darius's cock, pulling the minotaur's body forward toward his dripping pole. As it pressed overtop Clover's bobbing head, Darius peered at the flaring organ inches away from his mouth, then he inhaled it into his big bull mouth, sucking on it hungrily. Jessop groaned, placing his hands over the minotaur's horns, pulling his huge head harder down over his dick.

"Now that's what I call giving *head*," Bronwyn grinned as she rocked her hips harder against Tara's serpentine tail. "I'm so glad the three of you stumbled upon our camp. There's so many ways we can enjoy each other's company."

"Mmm," Tara nodded, as the snakes atop her head slithered down over the witch's neck, nipping on her nipples.

"Who knew screwing a *snake* could be this much fun?" Bronwyn smiled, pressing her fingers deeper into the side of Tara's twitching tail. "Shake that rattle inside me, bitch. I'm going to *come* watching the men empty their loads."

"Oh my God, Clover" Jessop groaned, rubbing his pole along Clover's back as Darius sucked the tip with his big bull mouth. "I'm rubbing my balls on your back while Darius sucks my dick. Just when I thought it couldn't get any better..."

"Are you enjoying getting sucked off by a man?" Bronwyn grinned, wrapping her legs tighter around Tara's tail, feeling her pleasure rising. "Maybe we should turn you into an animal more often..."

"I wouldn't say he's exactly a *man*," Jessop said, grunting harder as he approached the peak of his pleasure. "I don't think a normal man could suck my horse dick this way..."

"It looks like you're enjoying it nevertheless," the witch said, noticing Darius reaching over Tara's back with his hands to stroke Jessop's dick while he sucked on the end.

"He *does* seem a little more ambidextrous than a regular man," Jessop gasped, pulling Darius's horns harder against his twitching cock. "Oh my God, I'm going to come–"

"Yes, baby," Bronwyn said, watching Jessop's horse flanks pounding against the minotaur's face. "Come inside his mouth. This is even sexier than watching him *fuck* me."

"Oh fuckkk!" Jessop suddenly grunted, shaking his ass and emptying his enormous load inside Darius's mouth.

While he twitched against Clover's back, Darius started to stand up, lifting both Clover and Jessop off the log while he humped his hips wildly into Clover's face. She gagged as he rammed his entire length down her throat, and Bronwyn smiled watching his semen spilling out the sides of her mouth.

"Fuck, yes," she groaned, gripping Tara's tail harder between her legs. "I'm going to come baby. Twitch that rattle inside my hole. This feels so good."

While the snakes atop her head began squirming in a wild dance, Tara groaned, approaching her own orgasm.

"Unghh," she gasped. "My head feels like it's on fire."

"I think your babies are climaxing along with you," Bronwyn smiled. "That's the most expressive orgasm I've ever seen on a creature, human or animal."

"Holy *shit*," Clover panted as she disengaged from Darius's dick, watching the two girls twisting together in mutual ecstasy. "That rattle reminds me of one of my favorite toys from back home."

Bronwyn collapsed beside Tara as the snakes atop her head slithered over her neck and breasts.

"Where *is* this place you come from with such interesting toys?" she said.

"Somewhere far away from here," Clover chuckled. "Where we use *machines* to simulate sex with people instead of animals."

"You mean like *robots*?" the witch said. "Are they as sophisticated as my surrogates?"

"Not even close," Clover smiled, staring at Tara's flushed face as her tail twitched absentmindedly over the edge of the log.

"Maybe you can bring some ideas back to your people to develop new devices that mimic the characteristics of our *own* little toys?" Bronwyn said, smiling at Darius and Jessop.

"I'm already *on* it," Clover nodded, watching Tara's long serpent tongue flicking out of her mouth.

"How'd you like to switch places for a little while?" Bronwyn smiled. "I'm ready for some real *cock* for a change, and you look eager for a little girl-on-girl action."

"How long did you say it takes for everybody to transform back into their regular state?" Clover asked.

"Typically a day or two, but the more times they have sex, the faster they'll transform."

"We better get *busy* then," Clover smiled. "Before I lose my opportunity to have fun with Tara. I've never used a vibrator quite like that one before."

"And I've never had two cocks quite like *those* before," Bronwyn said, eyeing the men's twitching tools hungrily.

She walked over to the other side of the pit, pushing Darius gently down onto the ground as she straddled his hips and slid her wet pussy over his pole. While she leaned forward pressing her tits onto his muscular chest, she peered over her shoulder at Jessop, whose hard dick was flapping a few inches over her ass.

"Are you looking for another place to put that thing?" she smiled, winking up at him. "Because I think there's still one more that remains unserviced..."

"You mean...?" he said, staring at her pink pucker.

"Like your girlfriend said, we better make use of *every* opportunity we have while we still have time."

"Are you sure about this?" Jessop said, peering down at his giant horse dick and her tight sphincter. "I'm not sure it will fit–"

"You don't see me having any trouble taking Darius's *bull* cock, do you?" she smiled. "I'm a witch. You'd be surprised how versatile I can be when I'm properly motivated."

Jessop squatted his rear end down onto the ground then straddled Bronwyn and Darius with his front legs and Bronwyn reached behind her, grabbing the tip of his dick, rubbing it against her quivering anus. As he pushed gently forward, her hole slowly stretched until his flat head disappeared into her cavity.

"Holy fuck!" Jessop gasped.

"Is that tighter than your girlfriend's pussy?" Bronwyn grunted.

"Much," Jessop groaned.

"Don't stop there," Bronwyn moaned, beginning to rock her hips forward and back. "There's still a lot more room to maneuver. Can you feel Darius's dick rubbing inside me?"

"Yes," Jessop grunted. "This is something I've never felt before..."

"There are so many ways for you two boys to interact," she smiled. "You never know until you try."

"Nnngh," Jessop groaned, inching his dick further up the witch's butthole.

"Yes," she grunted. "Fuck my ass while I feel your dicks rubbing together inside me."

"I feel it," Jessop grunted. "I feel Darius's dick rubbing against mine while I fuck you..."

"Press it deeper," Bronwyn panted, pushing her hips back harder toward Jessop's flanks. "I want to feel your horse balls flapping against my ass."

"Oh *fuck*," Jessop hissed, sinking his dick all the way into Bronwyn's ass. "This feels incredible..."

While Bronwyn, Darius, and Jessop were joined together in a threesome, Clover and Tara were busy connecting in their own way. As Tara's twitching tongue snaked inside her mouth, the serpents atop her head caressed the sides of her face and neck while they kissed.

"What does it *feel* like to be in the body of a snake?" Clover asked.

"It's strange," Tara said, wrapping her tail around Clover's ass. "But I still feel like a girl on my upper half, and it's kind of fun caressing you with my other appendages."

"I like your talented *tongue* especially," Clover said, intertwining hers with Tara's as they probed each other's mouths.

"Would you like me to lick you a little lower?" Tara smiled.

"Oh my God," Clover panted, twisting her hips on the log. "I thought you'd never ask."

As Tara shifted her body lower, the snakes atop her head slithered over Clover's torso. While she fluttered her tongue over her nipples, the snakes encircled her breasts, stimulating every inch of her skin.

"Oh my God," Clover panted. "That feels incredible. Flick me with your snake tongue."

"Oh, I'm going to, believe me," Tara said, continuing to move lower as the snakes nibbled and caressed Clover's quivering stomach.

When she reached Clover's mound, they slithered between her legs, teasing the inside of her thighs and anus while Tara wrapped her tongue over Clover's hard clit.

"Holy shit, Tara," Clover whinnied. "I've never been sucked like this before. Suck my clit with your beautiful tongue. I can feel your hair stimulating my pussy..."

"Do you *still* want the witch to turn me back into my normal form as soon as possible?" Tara said, peering up at Clover between her legs.

"Maybe not for a little longer," Clover smiled, holding

her hands over Tara's head as the snakes wrapped around her wrists.

"Let's hope I don't revert back before you have another orgasm..."

"It won't take long if you keep doing *that*..."

While the snakes atop Tara's head began slithering into Clover's crease, nibbling and probing her two holes, they pressed inside each one, rolling and thrusting as Tara's tongue continued slapping against her twitching clit.

"Yes, Tara," Clover groaned. "Don't stop. I'm going to come so hard...

As she felt Tara's hair probing the inside of her pussy and anus, Clover glanced up hearing the trio on the other side of the pit beginning to growl in pleasure. While Jessop plowed his horse dick in and out of her bent-over ass, the two men's balls rubbed together under Bronwyn's quivering hips while she wailed in ecstasy as they emptied their seed deep inside her.

"Holy fuck!" Clover gasped, suddenly overtaken with the most powerful orgasm she'd ever felt. *"Ngahhh!"*

While she began to shake and twitch on the teetering log, Tara wrapped her tail around her hips to stabilize her as she jetted her juices all over Tara's face and twisting hair. When the group finally stopped shaking and pulled out from each other's holes, everybody peered at one another with contented expressions. Even Darius's bull face had a strange, almost human-like grin as he wiped the remains of Jessop's horse semen from the side of his lips with his human hands.

3

"So, what do you think?" Bronwyn said, peering over at Clover lying curled up in Tara's snake tail. "Is it as much fun playing with *my* sex toys as those fancy machines where you come from?"

"No comparison," Clover said, caressing Tara's breasts. "There's nothing like feeling a warm body reacting to my touch the same way I am to theirs."

"Even if it's a half-*animal* body?"

"As long as the important parts are on top," Clover smiled, leaning in to kiss Tara.

Bronwyn pinched her eyebrows together, not entirely sure what Clover meant.

"The important parts being–"

"A human face, lips, and brain. No offence to Darius, but I still like to imagine I'm having sex with a real person, even if the *rest* of them look like an animal."

"Speaking of..." the witch said. "You still haven't had your *own* turn seeing what it's like. If there's such a thing as reincarnation, how would you like to come back?"

Clover paused for a moment, reflecting back on one of her favorite animal movies.

"If it had to be in the form of an animal, I'd want it to be something strong and beautiful, but still with feminine features..."

Bronwyn walked over to her log, lifting her out of Tara's embrace. Then she ran her hands over Clover's naked body, pausing as she curved her palms over her muscular flanks, pulling one hand backwards like she was caressing a tail.

"Your wish is my command," she smiled, kissing Clover on the lips.

Suddenly, Clover's lower body began growing yellow fur while her hips pushed backwards into the body of a lion with a long tufted tail.

"A lion?" she said, peering at her sleek lower body.

"A *lioness*," Bronwyn said. "The perfect symbol of a strong, independent, female animal. And you still have your human parts on your upper half."

"This feels so strange..." Clover said, running her hands over the soft fur covering her hips. "Where's my–?"

"It's still there," the witch smiled. "Just a little further back. But don't worry, you still have your pretty tits and soft red hair."

"Mmm," Clover purred, feeling Bronwyn lower her head to suck on her nipples as her long locks spilled over the side of her face. "And they're just as sensitive as before. If the *rest* of my body parts feel this good when stimulated, I think I'm going to *enjoy* being part animal for a short while."

Bronwyn peered up, noticing Darius and Jessop staring hungrily at Clover's lion ass.

"Judging by the pheromones you're putting out to everyone in the camp, it looks you're ready to give them a try. Do you prefer a human dick or a horse dick?"

"I've already sampled Jessop's," Clover said, glancing over at their flapping hard-ons. "Plus my back's still aching from him propping his weight over my shoulders. Something tells me Darius's bull cock will be more than big enough to fill my hole."

"You heard the lady, Darius," Bronwyn smiled, motioning for her minotaur to join them. "It sounds like Clover isn't finished with you just yet."

Darius didn't waste any time loping up behind Clover, pushing her tail to the side. He peered down at her haunches finding her glistening slit then he positioned the tip of his tool over her opening, ramming his cock hard into her hole.

"Unghh!" Clover gasped, pushing the witch backwards from the force of his insertion.

"Well?" Bronwyn grinned, grasping Clover's torso while Darius began pounding her ass. "Do you think you made the right decision?"

"Choosing Darius, or fantasizing about being a *lion*?" Clover panted, feeling the minotaur's dick pushing deeper inside her.

"Both."

"His cock feels amazing inside me. It's true what Jessop said earlier. Animal sex is even more pleasurable than human sex. I feel like my entire lower body is on fire."

"Are you enjoying the attention on your *upper* body almost as much?" the witch smiled, rolling her tongue over Clover's hardening nipples.

"Yes," Clover groaned. "Suck my tits while Darius fucks my ass. It feels like I have two bodies, with twice the pleasure."

"You're not the *only* one feeling twice as aroused,"

Bronwyn said, glancing over at Tara and Jessop, who'd also joined the action in a similar bent-over position.

"How can I satisfy you?" Clover said, listening to her friends grunting along with her and Darius. "It's difficult for me to lick you in this position..."

Bronwyn lifted herself up a little higher and peered into Clover's eyes, then she hopped off the ground, wrapping her legs around Clover's lower torso. As she began humping her mound against Clover's lion breast, the two women moaned into each other's mouths, grinding their tits together in a tight embrace.

"Mhhh," Clover panted, feeling her lion pussy dripping onto the ground while Darius fucked her from behind.

"Can your human half process what's happening to your animal lower half?" Bronwyn smiled, looking into Clover's eyes while she pressed her clit harder against Clover's breastplate.

"Oh, it's *processing* alright," Clover huffed. "I can feel my climax building all the way from my ass to my ears. If my wetness is any sign of what's to come, I'm going to squirt all over Darius's tight balls like a firehose..."

"Yes, baby," Bronwyn hissed, clamping her legs tighter around Clover's flanks while she watched her minotaur pounding her ass. "Spray your lion juices all over his hard cock. I can see from the look on his face that he's about to come with you."

Suddenly, Darius snorted like he was charging a matador and he grasped Clover's flanks hard with his hands while he plowed his dick all the way inside her quivering pussy. When she heard him cumming, her tail slapped against his ass while she jetted her juices all over his balls and shaking legs. Moments later, Bronwyn joined the howling pair in simultaneous climax, shaking her pussy against Clover's front legs while she gasped into her mouth. Not long after, Jessop and Tara also began grunting and wailing while he thrust his horse dick into her ass. When everybody finished shaking and moaning, they collapsed onto the ground, totally spent and exhausted.

4

———

After everybody had a chance to recover, the three friends peered over at Bronwyn resting her head in Darius's lap.

"You've turned each of us into half-animal creatures," Tara said, slithering her tail seductively between the witch's legs. "But what about *you*? Have you ever experimented with trying it yourself?"

"I haven't had cause to so far," Bronwyn smiled, licking Darius's balls softly. "But then, I've never had this many subjects to play with at one time. The four of you are stretching me a little thin, bouncing from one person to another."

"Surely you could dream up some kind of animal composite that could satisfy *all* of us?" Tara said. "I mean, you're a witch after all."

"That I am," Bronwyn grinned, staring at everyone's newly tumescent sex organs. "It's not that I haven't thought about it. But now that I'm surrounded by so many tempting targets, you're giving me some new ideas..."

"Oh?" Clover said, shifting her body closer to Bronwyn. "What are you thinking?"

"Something that has both male and female body parts. With multiple appendages, so that I can service everyone at the same time."

"That sounds like the kind of sex toy I could warm up to," Clover purred, lapping Bronwyn's dripping pussy while the witch continued to formulate her plan.

Suddenly, Bronwyn's lower body began developing scales while her clit began to expand in Clover's mouth, extending out to the size of a huge, pulsing cock. At the same time, her lower body began stretching into the shape of a giant lizard as her neck split into three trunks in the shape of a hydra. But instead of a toothy dragon head atop each of her long necks, each branch had an exact duplicate of her pretty, purple-maned face.

"Holy shit!" Clover said, jumping backwards as the half-human/half-hydra creature raised up on its four legs, flapping its long tail from side to side. "You really *do* have a kinky imagination, don't you?"

"What can I say?" one of her heads smiled.

"People say variety is the spice of life," another head said.

"And I've always wanted to try it both ways," the third head grinned.

"Now it looks like you can have it *three* ways," Jessop said, his horse cock extending to its full length while he stared at the witch's three glistening mouths.

"And my necks are long enough to give your pole some *real* deep throat," she smiled. "Do you feel like giving it a try?"

"Fuck, yes," Jessop said, trotting over in front of the witch as his cock bobbed excitedly under his belly.

"Can you stand up so I can reach it more easily?" Bronwyn said.

"I'll try," Jessop said, raising his front hooves awkwardly in the air while trying to balance on his hind legs.

"That's better," Bronwyn smiled, seeing his horse dick rising to her face height.

"Now it's *your* turn, Darius," she said, motioning for her minotaur to join her at her side. "Stand beside Jessop so I can suck *both* of your cocks at the same time."

As Darius moved into position, Tara peered at the witch with the snakes atop her head writhing in excitement.

"What do you intend to do with your *third* head?" she said.

Bronwyn glanced under her flanks to check the size of her lizard penis.

"It looks like my cock is going to be too large to fit in your snake aperture. Why don't you lift your upper body up to my height while I play with your tits?"

"Okay, but what about–"

"All in due course, dear," the witch's faces grinned. "Now Clover, lay down on the grass like a good lioness while I fuck you from behind the way you were meant to be had. And while you're down there, maybe you can use your human appendages to stimulate your friend's pussy."

"Mmm," Clover purred, peering at Tara's dripping hole. "I was *wondering* when I was going to get a chance to lick her down there."

When the four of them assumed their positions in front of the hydra, Bronwyn's faces smiled a wicked grin as her mouths began to widen, engulfing the two men's huge organs all the way down to their balls. With her two heads busy sucking the men's giant dicks, she leaned forward with her third head to kiss Tara while Clover began licking her way up the snake's twitching tail. When she inserted her tongue into Tara's slit, Bronwyn's lizard body bent over her raised ass, plunging her big cock into Clover's dripping lion pussy. Tara gasped into the witch's mouth as the snakes atop her head began writhing from the pleasurable sensation they were receiving from her reproductive organ.

As the two women intertwined their lizard tongues, Bronwyn peered into Tara's eyes.

"Is Clover as skilled sucking a *snake* pussy as she is a human one?" she asked.

"Yes," Tara panted, while her snakes began squealing in ecstasy.

"How about you *boys*?" the witch asked. "Do you think an *animal* can give head as well as a human?"

"Better," Jessop grunted, plunging his horse cock deep down the hydra's undulating throat.

"Uhnn," Darius nodded, gripping the sides of her second head firmly with his two hands.

"What about you, Clover?" Bronwyn said, hearing her panting under her thrusting belly.

"Mhhh," Clover moaned, busy flicking her tongue into Tara's dripping snake slit.

"Sounds like you're all getting ready for some fireworks," the witch grinned. "I've never felt four people coming at the same time. Are you getting close?"

When everybody grunted in unison, Bronwyn pounded Clover's ass harder while she flicked her forked tongue out the side of her two heads, tickling the sensitive area behind the two men's tightening balls. As they began growling on the verge of climax, she lowered her other head to suck Tara's teats while the snakelets slithered over the witch's breasts, squeezing them in a tight grip.

With every one of them shaking on the verge of orgasm,

suddenly the entire forest was filled with the strange sound of five half-human/half-animal creatures climaxing at the same time. But this time, it took over a full minute for all of them to finish coming and emptying their loads inside their hosts. When they finally crumpled together into a twisted pile, Bronwyn pulled out her appendages, smiling at the group panting on the ground.

"Are you *still* sure you want to return to your human forms?" she grinned, licking the men's semen off the sides of her mouths.

5

———

"Let me tell you in a few minutes," Jessop said, rising up on his horse legs to head into the forest. "Right now, I need to take care of a different urge."

As Jessop trotted off into the woods to do his business, Clover peered up at the witch while she stroked Tara's scaly belly.

"As fun as this has been, I'm kind of missing my normal parts. It's strange seeing my friends in these weird animal bodies..."

"It shouldn't take long for your figures to return to their usual form," Bronwyn said. "Usually it takes a day or two, but at the rate we've been having sex, I expect it will happen any moment now–"

Suddenly, a loud howl came from the woods in the direction Jessop went, and everybody raised up with a startle.

"What was that?" Tara said, lifting her coiled snake body.

"It sounded like *Jessop*," Clover said. "Do you think he's in trouble?"

"I'm not sure," Tara said, slithering along the ground in his direction. "But in his present state, he doesn't have much protection. We better check up on him."

As the two girls headed into the brush in search of their friend, Darius looked at Bronwyn with a puzzled expression and she tilted her heads, motioning for him to follow them. When they reached a clearing in the thicket, they noticed Jessop crouched behind a fallen log, moving his hands tenderly over an arrow embedded in his flanks. Peering around, they noticed three hunters closing ranks toward him with bows raised, looking to finish him off.

Clover suddenly growled and darted toward one of the hunters, leaping on top of him with her lion body, clawing at his face with her large claws. At the same time, Tara slithered through the brush, wrapping her snake body around the second hunter's torso, tightening her grip as he struggled to breathe. Before the third hunter had a chance to react, Darius snuck up behind him, ramming him in the back with his horns. With the three hunters now immobilized and screaming for help, Bronwyn emerged in the clearing with her three faces peering the hunters curiously.

"What do we have here?" she said, tilting her heads at the captured quarry.

"What *are* you creatures!" one of the hunters said, peering at the five hybrid animals with wide eyes.

"Isn't it obvious?" one of Bronwyn's faces said with a sneer. "This one's a horse, that one's a lion and–."

"But how...?" the hunter said with a puzzled expression.

"I think that's the *last* thing you should be worried about right now," Bronwyn said, watching the trio pinning the hunters to the ground with their animal parts. "Why did you shoot one of our friends?"

"He...*it*...was roaming wild in the forest. We've never seen a centaur before. We thought it would be–"

"A *trophy* you could take back to your drinking buddies?" Bronwyn said. "Maybe something you could hang on your wall?"

"We didn't know–"

"That he was half *human*? What part of his human head and upper body did you miss? Did you think you could just kill *any* person willy-nilly in these parts?"

"We're sorry," the hunter gulped, trying to catch his breath while Tara constricted his chest more tightly with her tail. "We didn't realize you were together..."

"I *bet* you didn't," Bronwyn smiled. "And now the hunters have become the prey..."

"What should we do with them?" Clover said, peering down at the hunter pinned under her sharp claws.

"We shouldn't let them go right away," Bronwyn said. "They might bring more of their kind to stalk us. Let's bring them back to the camp and tie them up. I might be able to find something *else* to keep them amused for a little while."

"What about Jessop?" Tara said, watching him groan as he patted his inflamed lower flank gingerly.

"The wound doesn't look life-threatening," Bronwyn said. "It looks like the arrow struck next to his horse shoulder. We should be able to remove without too much difficulty. Are you still able to walk, Jessop?"

"I think so," he said, placing some pressure on his injured leg as he winced in pain.

"Let's return to the camp and see if we can patch you up," Bronwyn nodded. "The rest of you keep those hunters at bay until we make sure they're no longer a threat."

While Jessop rested his arm on Bronwyn's lizard body

for support, the group made their way back to the camp as Tara, Clover, and Darius held tightly onto the three hunters. When they returned to the fireside, they tied the hunters up to the side of a tree, then sat on a log to inspect Jessop's wound.

"Can you do anything to help him?" Clover said to Bronwyn, noticing the head of the arrow embedded about three inches under his skin.

"I don't have the power to remove the arrow directly," the witch said. "But maybe there's another way we can solve the problem."

As she began running her hands over his inflamed shoulder, Jessop's fur slowly began to turn back into human skin while his hind quarters retracted until he returned to his normal, upright human state. After a few more moments, the flesh around the arrow began to recede and the spear toppled to the ground, leaving a small scar on his hip.

"Jessop!" Clover said, throwing her arms around her friend. "You're finally back to normal! How do you feel?"

"A little strange," he said, peering down at his lower flanks. "And a little *smaller*..."

"You're still plenty man enough for me," Clover purred, caressing his flaccid penis softly.

"I'm not sure about that," he said, stroking her lion body. "I'm not exactly hung like a *horse* anymore, or a minotaur, or a giant lizard for that matter."

As he continued to stroke Clover softly, her fur began to revert to its natural skin while her lion body transformed back into her normal female figure.

"Mmm," he hummed, caressing her ass. "*That's* the Clover I remember."

"What about Tara?" Clover said, peering toward Bronwen. "How can we return *her* back to her normal state?"

"It looks like all it takes is a little healing touch," the witch smiled. "Why don't you try for yourself?"

As Clover and Jessop moved closer toward Tara, they began to stroke her tail and run their hands through her hair, and she began to slowly morph back into the figure of her five-foot-tall elf.

"Thank God," Clover smiled, kissing her friend on the lips. "As much fun as it was to feel you slithering all over me, I much prefer you like this."

"Me too," Tara said, lowering her hands between her legs to touch her throbbing pussy. "It feels good being able to spread my legs again to reach my sex. Being half snake has its advantages, but I'm glad I have my regular parts back."

The three friends peered over in the direction of Bronwyn and Darius, who were busy kissing one another. While her other heads started to retreat into her torso and her body began returning to it previous form, Darius's minotaur head suddenly started to shrink and transform into the shape of a man. When they finished reverting back to their previous forms, they disengaged, peering back at the others who'd been mesmerized watching the transformation.

"Wow," Tara said, staring at Darius's handsome man face with his chiseled cheekbones. "I can't imagine why you'd want to mess with that face."

"He *is* quite a stud, isn't he?" Bronwyn smiled, running her hands down over his washboard abs toward his still oversized cock.

"So what *now*?" Clover said, peering back at the hunters watching the group with their mouths agape.

"Well if you three think you've had enough of this whole

animal experience," Bronwyn grinned, "maybe I'll pick up with my new volunteers."

"Oh?" Clover said, still angry at them for what they tried to do to Jessop. "What exactly did you have in mind for them?"

"Something special..." Bronwyn nodded with a sly smile.

She nodded her head in their direction and the rope binding them together suddenly dropped to the base of the tree as they began morphing into miniature pigs.

"Three little pigs?" Clover chuckled, reflecting back on another one of her fairytale stories from back home. "Why that?"

"They can't do much harm in that state," Bronwyn smiled. "Plus, they're kind of cute, don't you think?"

"I suppose so, but they don't have any *human* parts left. What are you going to do with them?"

"I wouldn't feel too sorry for them," the witch smiled. "Did you know that pigs actually have the longest orgasm of any animal? Their climaxes can last over thirty minutes."

"Wow," Jessop said, noticing one of the pigs forming a long skinny erection under its belly as it tried to mount one of the other pigs.

"What about the *third* one?" he said, peering under its flanks to see if it was male or female.

"I don't know about *you* guys," Bronwyn smiled. "But I've worked up quite an appetite from all that animal sex. Would you like to stay for dinner? I could really go for some roast pork right about now."

Jessop turned to look at his two friends and they peered back at him with a wrinkled nose.

"I think it's time we continued on our way," Clover said. "Thanks for all the fun and games and for patching our friend back up. Perhaps we'll see you again somewhere in our travels."

"I'll look forward to it," Bronwyn smiled, grabbing the third pig by its tail. "You're not the *only* one who can dream up different ways to simulate sex with non-human objects."

R *eady for more erotic chills and thrills? Order the next exciting volume in Clover's Fantasy Adventures:*

Alcohol isn't the only kind of spirits served at the Cock and Hen bar...

ALSO BY VICTORIA RUSH

Wet your whistle a hundred different ways with Jade's Erotic Adventures. Browse the full collection of Victoria Rush steamy stories here:

Click to scan your favorites...

FOLLOW VICTORIA RUSH:

Want to keep informed of my latest erotic book releases? Sign up for my newsletter and receive a FREE bonus book:

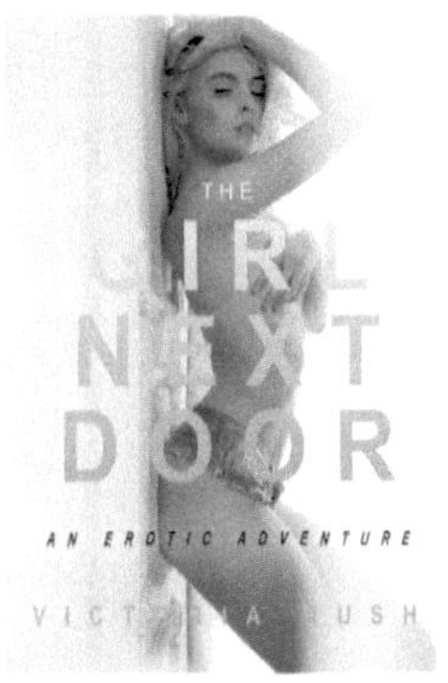

Spying on the neighbors just got a lot more interesting...